E       Kolanovic, Dubravka
Kol                            4881
        A special day

| DATE DUE | | $15.95 | |
|---|---|---|---|
| 9-27 | 4-3 | 2805 | |
| 10-5 | 4-9 | 42505 | |
| 10-14 | 4-19 | 42508 | |
| 11-4 | 10-15 | 42309 | |
| 11-24 | 11-1 | | |
| 1-27 | 11-14 | | |
| 9-26 | 12-6 | | |
| 10-3 | 3-5 | | |
| 10-19 | 3-22 | | |
| 1-04 | 4-4 | | |
| 1-15 | 12-24 | | |
| 3-27 | 9-23 | | |

**WITHDRAWN**

# A SPECIAL DAY

# A SPECIAL DAY

### written & illustrated by
# DUBRAVKA KOLANOVIĆ

## LANDMARK EDITIONS, INC.

P.O. Box 4469 • 1402 Kansas Avenue • Kansas City, Missouri 64127
(816) 241-4919

Dedicated to
my mom and dad;
and to all small children
in Croatia who are
suffering from war.

COPYRIGHT © 1993  DUBRAVKA KOLANOVIĆ

International Standard Book Number: 0-933849-45-1(LIB.BDG.)

Library of Congress Cataloging-in-Publication Data
Kolanović, Dubravka, 1973-
    A special day / written and illustrated by Dubravka Kolanović.
    p.      cm.
    Summary:  A young boy enjoys a visit with his grandparents at their
house in the woods, where he meets a friendly, hungry bear.
    ISBN 0-933849-45-1 (lib.bdg. : acid-free paper)
    [1. Grandparents—Fiction.            2. Bears—Fiction.]

    I. Title.
PZ7.K8315Sp          1993
[E]—dc20                                        93-13419
                                                CIP
                                                AC

Editorial Coordinator:  Nancy R. Thatch
Creative Coordinator:  David Melton

Printed in the United States of America

Landmark Editions, Inc.
P.O. Box 4469
1402 Kansas Avenue
Kansas City, Missouri 64127
(816) 241-4919

# A SPECIAL DAY

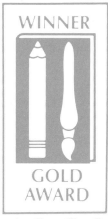

WINNER

GOLD AWARD

1992

In 1992, without any intention on the part of Landmark, our NATIONAL WRITTEN & ILLUSTRATED BY...AWARDS CONTEST FOR STUDENTS went international. A sixteen-year-old Canadian boy, Travis Williams, won in the 14 to 19 age category. Another outstanding book in that category also received the attention and admiration of our judges. That book, A SPECIAL DAY, was created by a young woman from Croatia, who was attending school in North Carolina as a foreign exchange student. Our editors at Landmark were pleased to present a special Gold Award for literary and artistic achievement to the book's author and illustrator, eighteen-year-old Dubravka Kolanović.

You will not have to look at more than a couple of pages of A SPECIAL DAY to understand why our editors were so impressed with Dubravka's work. She has the ability to create extraordinary images in line and color. And she has a fully developed, clearly defined style of illustrating that is truly outstanding in one so young.

Dubravka dazzles our eyes with colors and fluid shapes. The backgrounds of her beautiful illustrations explode on the pages with vivid colors, while the central characters are all presented in black and white. The people and animals which Dubravka creates are not mere cartoon characters; they are thoughtful characterizations that have unique and complete personalities of their own.

As you will see, A SPECIAL DAY is a sweet book. The humor is warm and subtle. The people are nice and the animals are nice. And there are no villains and no clashes of wills. It is a very simple story about a young boy named Ivan who goes to visit his grandparents. During one special day, they enjoy the pleasures of a walk in the woods, a swim in a lake, fishing in a stream, and taking wild raspberries home to eat.

I like Cat, Dog, and Bear. They make me smile. Young children are sure to love this delightful book! I think adults will like it, too.

— David Melton
Creative Coordinator
Landmark Editions, Inc.

Today is a special day.  Ivan is so excited.
For the first time, he is riding on a train all by himself.
He is going to visit his grandpapa and his grandmamma
who live in the country.

The train pulls into the station.

Grandpapa and Grandmamma have smiles on their faces.

They greet Ivan with hugs and kisses.

Dog wants to give Ivan a kiss too — "SLURP! SLURP!"

Grandpapa's car zooms over the mountain road.
Ivan loves the up-and-down, roller-coaster ride!
He can hardly wait to get to the house in the woods
where Grandpapa and Grandmamma live.
Bear always seems to know when Ivan is coming to visit.

Grandmamma makes pancakes for lunch.
Ivan thinks she makes the
best pancakes in the whole world.
He is so hungry, he will eat three or four.

Grandpapa may eat five or six.

Cat likes pancakes.  But she likes milk better.

Bear likes pancakes too.

Bear is always hungry.

4881

Ivan goes for a walk
with Grandpapa and Grandmamma.
Dog and Cat follow close behind.
Ivan wants to swim in the mountain stream.
"I'll race you to the other side!" he calls.
Ivan is a fast swimmer.

Grandpapa and Grandmamma can swim even faster.
But when they race with Ivan, they always let him win.
Bear does not like to race.
Bear likes to float on his back
and splash his feet in the cool water.

Grandmamma picks wild raspberries in the woods.
Ivan and Grandpapa fish in the sparkling stream.
"What a lucky day," says Grandpapa.
"We are catching many, many fish."
Bear is glad to hear that.
He hopes there will be an extra fish for him.
Bear loves fresh fish.

As they walk home, Grandpapa tells Ivan
about all the animals that live in the woods.
While Grandpapa talks and talks, Ivan is busy.
He is picking up chestnuts
that have fallen from the trees.
Bear is busy too — "YUM! YUM!"

Ivan carves a horse from one of the chestnuts.
Grandpapa and Grandmamma
think the carving is beautiful.
"Young carvers and old fishermen get hungry,"
says Grandpapa. "We need some food to eat."

"Then you wash the raspberries,"
Grandmamma tells him.

"Ivan and I will go to the pantry to get flour and sugar."

"Raspberry is my favorite kind of pie," says Ivan.

Bear likes raspberry pie too.

Ivan likes to go to the pantry with Grandmamma.
There are baskets filled with apples
and sacks full of potatoes and onions.
There are plump sausages hanging from a line.

And there are…*FIVE MICE!*

"Get out of my pantry!" screams Grandmamma.

Bear hopes to visit the pantry someday.

Bear likes sausages too.

Outside, the wind begins to blow.
Storm clouds grumble. Lightning flashes.
And rain starts to fall.
"Grandpapa, are you scared?" asks Ivan.
"No," answers Grandpapa.
"Our little house is very strong.
We are safe from the storm."

Ivan tries to be brave.  Bear tries to be brave too.
But when lightning flashes and thunder claps,
Bear hides under the porch.
Bear wishes he could be inside the snug little house.

Soon the storm is over.
Ivan, Grandpapa, and Grandmamma
enjoy a delicious meal.
And for dessert… they have raspberry pie!
Suddenly Ivan stops eating.
"What is scratching at the door?" he asks.
"It is only Bear," answers Grandpapa.
"Maybe Bear is hungry," says Ivan.
"Bear is *always* hungry," replies Grandmamma.
"Poor Bear," says Ivan.

That night Grandpapa and Grandmamma
dream of chestnut horses, wild raspberries,
and their special day with Ivan.
But Ivan cannot sleep.
He gets out of bed and tiptoes down the stairs.

He puts a big slice of raspberry pie on a plate.
Then he opens the back door
and places the pie on the porch.
"Good night, Bear," whispers Ivan.

A Chandrasekhar
age 9

Anika Thomas
age 13

Cara Reichel
age 15

Jonathan Kahn
age 9

Adam Moore
age 9

Leslie A MacKeen
age 9

Elizabeth Haidle
age 13

Amy Hagstrom
age 9

Isaac Whitlatch
age 11

Dav Pilkey
age 19

**by Aruna Chandrasekhar, age 9**
Houston, Texas

A touching and timely story! When the lives of many otters are threatened by a huge oil spill, a group of concerned people come to their rescue. Wonderful illustrations.
Printed Full Color
ISBN 0-933849-33-8

**by Anika D. Thomas, age 13**
Pittsburgh, Pennsylvania

A compelling autobiography! A young girl's heartrending account of growing up in a tough, inner-city neighborhood. The illustrations match the mood of this gripping story.
Printed Two Colors
ISBN 0-933849-34-6

**by Cara Reichel, age 15**
Rome, Georgia

Elegant and eloquent! A young stonecutter vows to create a great statue for his impoverished village. But his fame almost stops him from fulfilling that promise.
Printed Two Colors
ISBN 0-933849-35-4

**by Jonathan Kahn, age 9**
Richmond Heights, Ohio

A fascinating nature story! Patulous, a prairie rattlesr searches for food, he must t avoid the claws and fangs of his enemies.
Printed Full Color
ISBN 0-933849-36-2

**by Adam Moore, age 9**
Broken Arrow, Oklahoma

A remarkable true story! When Adam was eight years old, he fell and ran an arrow into his head. With rare insight and humor, he tells of his ordeal and his amazing recovery.
Printed Two Colors
ISBN 0-933849-24-9

**by Michael Aushenker, age 19**
Ithaca, New York

Chomp! Chomp! When Arthur forgets to feed his goat, the animal eats everything in sight. A very funny story — good to the last bite. The illustrations are terrific.
Printed Full Color
ISBN 0-933849-28-1

**by Leslie Ann MacKeen, age 9**
Winston-Salem, North Carolina

Loaded with fun and puns! When Jeremiah T. Fitz's car stops running, several animals offer suggestions for fixing it. The results are hilarious. The illustrations are charming.
Printed Full Color
ISBN 0-933849-19-2

**by Elizabeth Haidle, age 13**
Beaverton, Oregon

A very touching story! The gr iest Elfkin learns to cheris friendship of others after he an injured snail and befrien orphaned boy. Absolutely bea
Printed Full Color
ISBN 0-933849-20-6

**by Amy Hagstrom, age 9**
Portola, California

An exciting western! When a boy and an old Indian try to save a herd of wild ponies, they discover a lost canyon and see the mystical vision of the Great White Stallion.
Printed Full Color
ISBN 0-933849-15-X

**by Isaac Whitlatch, age 11**
Casper, Wyoming

The true confessions of a devout vegetable hater! Isaac tells ways to avoid and dispose of the "slimy green things." His colorful illustrations provide a salad of laughter and mirth.
Printed Full Color
ISBN 0-933849-16-8

**by Dav Pilkey, age 19**
Cleveland, Ohio

A thought-provoking parable! Two kings halt an arms race and learn to live in peace. This outstanding book launched Dav's career. He now has seven more books published.
Printed Full Color
ISBN 0-933849-22-2

**by Karen Kerber, age 12**
St. Louis, Missouri

A delightfully playful book! Th is loaded with clever alliteration gentle humor. Karen's bright ored illustrations are compos wiggly and waggly strokes of g
Printed Full Color
ISBN 0-933849-29-X

*Your Students Will Love These Wonderful Book*

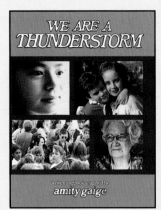

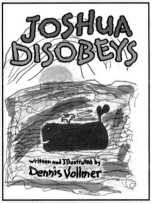

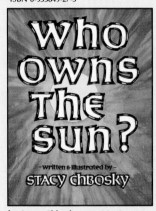

# THE WINNERS OF THE 1992 NATIONAL
# WRITTEN & ILLUSTRATED BY... AWARDS FOR STUDENTS

**FIRST PLACE**
6–9 Age Category
**Benjamin Kendall**
age 7
State College, Pennsylvania

**FIRST PLACE**
10–13 Age Category
**Steven Shepard**
age 13
Great Falls, Virginia

**FIRST PLACE**
14–19 Age Category
**Travis Williams**
age 16
Sardis, B.C., Canada

**GOLD AWARD**
Publisher's Selection
**Dubravka Kolanovic'**
age 18
Savannah, Georgia

**GOLD AWARD**
Publisher's Selection
**Amy Jones**
age 17
Shirley, Arkansas

  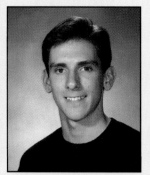  

### ALIEN INVASIONS

When Ben puts on a new super-hero costume, he starts seeing Aliens who are from outer space. His attempts to stop the pesky invaders provide loads of laughs. The colorful illustrations add to the fun!

29 Pages, Full Color
ISBN 0-933849-42-7

### FOGBOUND

A gripping thriller!
When a boy rows his boat to an island to retrieve a stolen knife, he must face threatening fog, treacherous currents, and a sinister lobsterman.
Outstanding illustrations!

29 Pages, Two-Color
ISBN 0-933849-43-5

### CHANGES

A chilling mystery!
When a teen-age boy discovers his classmates are missing, he becomes entrapped in a web of conflicting stories, false alibis, and frightening changes.
Dramatic ink drawings!

29 Pages, Two-Color
ISBN 0-933849-44-3

### A SPECIAL DAY

Ivan enjoys a wonderful day in the country with his grandparents, a dog, a cat, and a delightful bear that is *always* hungry. Cleverly written, brilliantly illustrated! Little kids will love this book!

29 Pages, Full Color
ISBN 0-933849-45-1

### ABRACADABRA

A whirlwind adventure!
An enchanted unicorn helps a young girl rescue her eccentric aunt from the evil Sultan of Zabar. A charming story, with lovely illustrations that add a magical glow!

29 Pages, Full Color
ISBN 0-933849-46-X

## BOOKS FOR STUDENTS BY STUDENTS!

# Written & Illustrated by...
## by David Melton

This highly acclaimed teacher's manual offers classroom-proven, step-by-step instructions in all aspects of teaching students how to write, illustrate, assemble, and bind original books. Loaded with information and positive approaches that really work. Contains lesson plans, more than 200 illustrations, and suggested adaptations for use at all grade levels — K through college.

**The results are dazzling!**
Children's Book Review Service, Inc.

**WRITTEN & ILLUSTRATED BY...** provides a current of enthusiasm, positive thinking and faith in the creative spirit of children. David Melton has the heart of a teacher.
THE READING TEACHER

**...an exceptional book!** Just browsing through it stimulates excitement for writing.
Joyce E. Juntune, Executive Director
The National Association for Creativity

**A "how to" book that really works.**
Judy O'Brien, Teacher

a revolutionary two-brain approach for teaching students how to write and illustrate amazing books

**David Melton**

Softcover, 96 Pages
ISBN 0-933849-00-1

# LANDMARK EDITIONS, INC.
### P.O. BOX 4469 • KANSAS CITY, MISSOURI 64127 • (816) 241-4919